To my family—thanks for putting up with my long hours at the keyboard
—D. D. M.

Off to Bethlehem!
Text copyright © 2002 by Dandi Daley Mackall
Illustrations copyright © 2002 by R. W. Alley
Printed in the U.S.A. All rights reserved.
HarperCollins®, ☀®, and HarperFestival® are registered trademarks of HarperCollins Publishers Inc.
Library of Congress catalog card number: 00-057221
www.harperchildrens.com
Typography by Max Maslansky

Off to Bethlehem!

By Dandi Daley Mackall
Illustrated by R. W. Alley

HarperFestival®
A Division of HarperCollinsPublishers

Today's the day!
Don't delay!
Donkey's running all the way!

Trotting fast,
Time at last,
Off to Bethlehem!

Crowded streets,
Frantic spin,
Rambling, scrambling
Inn to inn!

Stable bare,
Creatures share,
Here in Bethlehem.

Wintry sky,
    Angels nigh,
Singing, shouting, "Praise on high!"

Heralding,
    Fluttering,
Off to Bethlehem!

Shepherds hear,
    Shepherds fear,
Rushing on a midnight clear!

No more sleep!
Herding sheep,
Off to Bethlehem!

Cows and sheep
Bounce and leap,
Racing in a hillside sweep!

Nuzzling,
Cantering,
Off to Bethlehem!

Brightest star,
　　Promised star,
　　Kings on camels riding far—

Following,
    Galloping,
        Off to Bethlehem!

Come and see!
   Majesty!
Journeys end on bended knee.

Marveling,
   Worshiping,
Here in Bethlehem.

Wondrous sight,
   God's own light,
Christ the King is born this night!

Go and tell—
   All is well . . .
Here in Bethlehem!